M.J.MISRA

EGMONT

For Ali Dougal, a brilliant editor

EGMONT

We bring stories to life

Dinosaur Land: Sky High!
First published in Great Britain 2013
by Egmont UK Limited
The Yellow Building
1 Nicholas Road
London W11 4AN

ISBN 978 1 4052 6476 1
1 3 5 7 9 10 8 6 4 2

www.egmont.co.uk
www.michellemisra.com

A CIP catalogue record for this title is available from the British Library

Printed and bound in Great Britain by CPI Group (UK) Ltd,
Croydon, CR04YY

53481/1

CONTENTS

Meadow Farm Park

Max Jordan smiled as he watched the barn owl stretch out a silvery-white wing. *He looks a lot happier now*, Max thought. The bird was standing on a wooden perch. Its other wing was injured and strapped to its side.

As the owl ruffled its feathers, Max looked over at his mum, leaning beside him on the fence at Meadow Farm Park. Max's parents were vets and had been called out to help with the owl. It was the weekend, so Max had been able to come too.

'How could he have broken his wing?' Max asked his mum.

'Anything could have happened,' his mum said. 'A car could have hit him while he was out hunting, or he might have flown into a low-lying building.'

It's lucky someone found him,' said Max.

'Very lucky,' said Mrs Jordan. 'If he hadn't been brought here he'd probably have died. Now, come on – Jenny, the farm park owner, said we could have a look around.'

Max jumped down from the fence. 'Will the splint have to be on his wing for long?' he asked as they set off.

'Not too long, hopefully,' said Mrs Jordan. 'Three weeks tops.'

Three weeks seemed like ages to Max. 'I really wouldn't want to be in plaster for all that time.'

'If you broke your arm, you'd have to be,' said Mrs Jordan. 'I know it's not very nice for him right now but at least he'll get better and then be able to fly again.'

'Imagine if a flying dinosaur broke its wing and you had to put *it* in plaster,' said Max as they walked over to a wooden hen house, near to a pond.

'Oh, Max,' his mum laughed. 'You're obsessed! I'm not quite sure how you jumped from an owl to a dinosaur.'

'Well, because birds are descended from dinosaurs,' Max said.

His mum looked surprised for a moment. 'You know, I'd forgotten that.'

Max loved dinosaurs and had read lots of dinosaur fact books. 'The weird thing is that birds aren't descended from pterosaurs – the flying dinosaurs,' he said. 'They're actually related to the dinosaurs who lived on the ground, like the T-Rex.'

'I think you must know everything there is to know about dinosaurs!' his mum said, shaking her head. 'It's a pity there aren't any left for you to meet.'

Max hid a smile. He had a special secret: he owned a magic fossil that could take him to a land where dinosaurs still existed! He'd made two friends there – Fern and her dad, Adam. They looked after sick and injured dinosaurs, and whenever they needed help, the fossil would whisk Max away

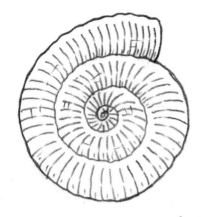

to Dinosaur Land. The fossil was in his pocket now. He carried it everywhere – even the bath! He thought about Dinosaur Land with its wide plains, lush forest and smoking volcanoes . . .

'Hey, Mum,' he said suddenly. 'What do you think the dinosaur said when he saw the volcano explode?'

His mum raised her eyebrows. 'I don't

know, what did the dinosaur say?'

Max grinned. 'What a lava-ly day. Get it?'

Max's mum laughed again. 'Your jokes get worse and worse!'

They reached the henhouse. A mother hen was clucking around outside it with her brood. 'Look at all those sweet little chicks,' Max's mum said. 'It's very hard to believe they might be related to an enormous T-Rex!'

Max nodded. He'd never met a T-Rex

but he had come face-to-face with some other meat-eating dinosaurs and they were seriously scary. Nothing like the cute little bundles of feathers who were scratching around in the grass here.

'Why is one of the chicks different?' he asked, spotting a little muddy brown bird amongst all the yellow ones.

'Because that's a duckling, not a chick!' The voice came from behind them.

Max and his mum turned. Jenny, the park owner, was coming towards them. 'The duckling's mother died,' she explained. 'So the mother hen has been looking after it – she's its foster mum.'

'Hens make great foster mothers, don't

they?' said Max's mum.

'Oh, yes,' agreed Jenny. 'And the babies just seem to attach themselves to whoever they *think* is their mum, even if they look nothing like her.'

It's the same with dinosaurs, Max thought. In Dinosaur Land, he had met a baby allosaurus that had been fostered by a triceratops.

'I had a hen foster an owl chick once!' said Jenny. 'The only problem was that the owl chick wouldn't fly until I put it back with other owls.'

Max peered into the pen. 'What's that chick doing?' he asked curiously. 'That one over there.' He pointed at one that was fluffing up its feathers and raising its wings.

'That's just the way it greets its mum,' Jenny explained. She turned to Max's mum. 'Before you go could you take a quick look at one of the sheep?'

'Sure.' Mrs Jordan looked at Max. 'Do you

want to wait here for me, or come?'

'I'll wait here,' Max said. He was keen to watch the chicks. He turned to look at the water. The duckling pottered down the slope towards the pond. It reached the edge and pecked at the water. It looked very excited. Then it fluffed up its wings and jumped in! The mother hen gave a squawk of horror and charged down to the water's edge. She stood there, clucking in alarm as she watched the duckling paddle around.

Hens didn't swim and the mother obviously thought the duckling had gone crazy! She looked very worried.

Max wondered if he should do something. He hated seeing the mother hen so upset. But suddenly a humming sound filled the air and his pocket felt very warm. He reached inside. The magic fossil was glowing! Max gasped. He must be off to Dinosaur Land again!

Bath Time!

Max found himself spinning in a tunnel of colours, tumbling over and over until he didn't know which way was up and which was down. Then . . . THUD! He landed on solid ground.

Max rubbed his eyes and looked around. Normally when he arrived in Dinosaur

Land he was out on the open plains, but this time he was inside the sanctuary, near to the little white stone house where Fern and her dad lived. He stared in wonder as he saw that there were winged dinosaurs

everywhere! Each one was about the size of a massive seagull with a light-coloured body, long arms, and a leathery tail and wings. *Pterodactyls!* Max realized. They were making squawking, shrieking sounds.

Max could barely hear himself think above all the noise. He scrambled to his feet.

'Max!'

Hearing his name, Max turned and saw Fern and Adam standing by a stone trough. They were bathing two pterodactyls! He hurried over.

'Hi! What's happening here?'

'Oh, Max!' cried Fern. 'I'm so glad you've come!'

'Yes, we could really use another pair of

hands,' said Adam. He was a tall man, with friendly eyes and dark curly hair like Fern's.

Max saw that the pterodactyls around him had sticky grey stuff clinging to their bodies and wings. 'What's that?' he asked curiously.

'It's lava. They got caught in it as it was cooling after coming out of the volcano.' Fern explained. 'Dad found them and brought them into the sanctuary to get cleaned. If they're not clean they can't fly.'

'A bit like seagulls when they get stuck in tar,' said Max.

'Sea . . . *what?*' said Fern, puzzled.

'Seagulls,' said Max. 'They're a type of white bird from my world. They live by the sea and catch fish.'

'What are birds?' Fern frowned as she held a baby pterodactyl upside down by its legs.

'Things that fly,' said Max. 'A bit like pterodactyls.' He always forgot that birds and animals from his world didn't exist in Dinosaur Land. 'So, can I help you with what you're doing?'

'Yes, please!' said Adam. 'The quicker we can get them clean and back into the sky, the better.'

Max rolled up his sleeves. Copying Fern, he approached the nearest pterodactyl. He grabbed its long sharp beak with one hand, holding it shut, and picked the creature up by its legs. Then he popped it into the

trough and started rinsing it all over. The pterodactyl struggled but Max was firm and soon the sticky substance was all gone. He let the pterodactyl go and it hopped off across the ground before spreading its wet wings, flapping them hard and soaring up into the sky.

'I'll go and get us all a drink,' said Adam after they had been washing and cleaning for a while. 'This is thirsty work!'

Max wiped his arm across his forehead. It was a hot, sunny day and he was feeling thirsty too.

'So, how's everything been here?' he asked Fern as Adam went off towards the stone house.

'Good,' said Fern, brushing back a strand of curly black hair that had fallen into her eyes. 'Red and Algie are still living happily out in the wild.'

Max smiled as he remembered the stegosaurus and the lambeosaurus he had met on his last visit.

'And how about Trixie?' he asked, thinking of the big friendly einiosaurus they sometimes rode on the back of.

'She's fine,' said Fern. 'You'll have to come and see her later once we've got these pterodactyls cleaned.' She grinned as the baby pterodactyl flew up on to Max's left shoulder. 'Ha! Looks like you've made a friend!'

Max stroked the pterodactyl's head. It made a little crooning noise and rubbed its beak against his fingers. It was very small compared to the others – only about the size of a little parrot.

'Caaark!' it cawed.

Max thought of a joke. 'Hey, what do you get when a pterodactyl bites your arm?'

'It hasn't, has it?' Fern asked, looking at the pterodactyl in alarm.

'No, don't worry!' Max laughed. 'It's just a joke.'

'Phew!' said Fern. 'OK, so what *do* you get when a pterodactyl bites your arm?'

'A dino-sore,' Max grinned. 'Get it?'

Fern giggled. 'That's a terrible joke, Max, but you know something? I'm really glad you're back here to make me laugh! It's much more fun when you're visiting.'

The pterodactyl nibbled Max's ear.

'Ow!' protested Max. He gave the baby a gentle push. 'Stop eating me and fly away!'

But the baby didn't move. Max carefully took it from his shoulder and placed it on the ground. 'Go on!' he encouraged, shooing at it with his hands. But the pterodactyl just bobbed up and down and then it started to walk towards Max on all fours, its wings tucked into its back.

'Caaaaarrrk,' it said hopefully.

'I wonder where its mum is,' said Fern, frowning.

At that moment, Adam appeared, walking down the path with a jug of star-fruit lemonade and some stone beakers. 'Here we are!' he called out.

They hurried over to him. Fern poured out the lemonade and they gulped it down greedily.

'Yum. Delicious!' said Max.

As the three of them drank, most of the

pterodactyls started to fly away but the little one was still hopping around them.

'Caaaaarrrk,' it said insistently, staring at Max with its bright black eyes.

'It seems to really like Max, Dad,' said Fern. 'It keeps following him.'

'It's not an it – he's a boy!' said Adam.

'Well, it . . . I mean, he, doesn't seem to know what to do with himself,' said Max.

The little pterodactyl stopped by Max's feet and held up his wing.

'Perhaps he's broken his wing,' said Fern suddenly. 'Maybe that's why he's not flying away.'

Max felt a jolt of alarm.

'It seems unlikely,' said Adam, putting down his cup. 'But I'd better take a look . . .'

A New Friend

Adam ran his hand along the length of the baby pterodactyl's wings. Then he felt underneath its arms and checked it all over before finally placing it back down on the ground.

'Well, he seems to be all right,' he said. 'There's nothing broken.'

'Oh . . .' Max and Fern looked puzzled. It was good news, of course, but it didn't explain why the pterodactyl wouldn't leave Max and join its flock.

The pterodactyl lifted its wings – both of them this time.

'What's he doing?' Fern asked.

Max remembered the chick at the farm that morning. 'Back in my world, a baby chick does that to greet its mum.'

Fern started to giggle as she looked from

the pterodactyl to Max.

'What's so funny?' asked Max.

'Perhaps he thinks *you're* his mum,' said Fern.

'No, why . . .' began Max – but, now that he looked again, the pterodactyl was gazing very lovingly at him! And as he walked back across the ground, the pterodactyl followed him. Max changed direction and the little pterodactyl did too. When Max stood on one leg, the pterodactyl did the same, cocking

its head on one side as it copied Max.

Fern and Adam both snorted with laughter. 'He *does* think you're his mum!' Fern exclaimed.

Max's shocked expression made Fern and Adam laugh even harder.

'Oh, dear.' Adam wiped his eyes. 'This really isn't funny. If the pterodactyl won't fly away, he'll be an easy target for large predators.'

Max frowned. He didn't want the dinosaur

to be in danger. 'Go on, shoo. Go after your flock . . .' He ran at it and tried to get it to fly up into the sky.

The pterodactyl let out another plaintive 'Caaaark'.

Max groaned. 'How do you get a pterodactyl to fly when it doesn't want to?'

'Is that a joke?' asked Fern.

'If only!' sighed Max as he looked at the baby.

The pterodactyl hopped up and down on the spot, as if he was trying to fly. He managed to get as high as Max's shoulders but then seemed happy to rest there.

Max looked at Adam and Fern. 'What are we going to do?'

'Perhaps if we leave him here he'll get bored and fly after the others,' Adam suggested. 'Put him on the ground and come with me. I've got something I really want to show you. You might be just the person to help me with it.'

'Cool,' said Max.

'It's not a dinosaur,' said Fern. 'It's one of Dad's new inventions!' She shook her head. 'It's not working properly and he's been driving me mad with it.'

'What is it?' said Max, intrigued.

'Step this way,' said Adam, 'and all will be revealed!'

As Max went to follow Adam and Fern, the pterodactyl squawked anxiously and chased after him. He managed to take off into the air, just enough to fly right back on to Max's shoulder.

'Looks like you're going nowhere without him!' Adam shook his head. 'Hopefully he'll lose interest soon. In the meantime, you'd better give him a name.'

'Um, well . . .' Max looked thoughtful. What sort of name would suit the little creature? And then it came to him. 'Reg,' Max grinned. 'I think I'll call him Reg.'

'Right then,' said Adam. 'Reg it is! Now, come on, follow me . . .'

An Invention!

'And there we have it!' Adam said proudly.
'My new invention!'

Max stared at the large structure in front
of him. A wooden stake had been hammered
into the ground and a round wheel was
attached to the top of it. Half a dozen
sails made out of sackcloth were sticking

out from the wheel. They weren't moving,
despite the breeze.

'Have you ever seen anything like it
before?' asked Fern.

'Well, yes, I have actually,' admitted Max. 'We have things like that in my world – they're called windmills.'

'*Windmills . . .*' said Adam, trying out the new word. 'That's a good name! Are they just like this one?'

'Kind of,' said Max hesitantly. 'Only in my world, the sails turn round.'

'That's exactly what I was hoping for,' said Adam, prodding the lifeless sails. 'There's plenty of wind, but they just won't turn. I can't understand it. Do you have any idea why they won't work, Max?'

Max wanted to help but he didn't really know much about windmills. 'I'm not sure,' he said. 'I'm sorry.'

Adam sighed. 'Oh, dear. I was hoping you might be able to tell me something from your world that would give me a clue.'

'Why do you want a windmill anyway?' Max asked curiously.

'Dad wants to use it to pump water from

the well,' Fern explained.

'I thought that if there was ever a drought it would be good to be able to get water quickly,' said Adam.

Max could see how useful that would be for the dinosaur sanctuary. He looked at the windmill again. 'I'll keep thinking about why it's not working,' he promised.

'Thank you,' said Adam, brightening up. 'You've always been such a great help in the past. It would be wonderful if you could help me with this too. Now, how about you two keep an eye on things here for me while I ride Trixie out on to the plains and check that all the dinosaurs there are OK.'

'Sure,' said Max.

Reg bobbed up and down on Max's shoulder and gave a little 'Caaaark!'.

'Reg says he'll help!' grinned Fern.

'What are we going to do about him?' wondered Adam.

'Can't he just stay with us, Dad?' Fern

pleaded. 'At least for a bit.'

Adam scratched his chin. 'I don't know, Fern. It's important that he doesn't get too tame. If he does he won't be able to survive in the wild.'

'Well, why don't we just let him stay while we teach him how to fly properly again,' said Fern.

'All right,' Adam agreed. 'He can stay for a while. We can have a go at teaching him to fly when I get back from the plains.'

'Thanks, Dad,' said Fern, giving him a hug.

'In the meantime there's some lunch in the house,' said Adam. 'Help yourselves.'

As Adam disappeared off down the little path, Fern turned back to Max. 'You know, this is the third project that Dad's started. None of them ever get finished. I really hope you can work out what's going wrong with the windmill.'

'It's strange,' said Max, looking thoughtful.

'Something doesn't look quite right.' He felt an idea flicker in his mind, but just then Reg prodded him with his beak and the idea vanished. 'What is it?' he said to the little dinosaur.

The pterodactyl snapped his beak open and shut several times.

Fern frowned. 'What's he doing?'

'I think he's hungry,' realised Max. His own tummy gave a loud rumble and he laughed. 'He's not the only one!'

Fern grinned. 'Let's go and have some lunch. I'm sure we can find some fish in the house for Reg too.'

It was cool inside and Max was glad for a chance to sit down. Reg perched on the wooden table beside him.

Fern fetched a piece of fish for the pterodactyl and put it on a stone plate. Reg didn't touch it, but as Max started to eat the bread and cream cheese that Adam had left out, Reg opened his mouth hopefully. Max ignored him so Reg edged closer and squawked loudly. *Snap, snap,* his beak went and his dark eyes bored into Max.

Fern started to giggle. 'Oh, no!'

'What?' Max said.

'Um . . . you know how he thinks you're his mum?'

'Yes,' Max answered warily.

'Well, do you know how pterodactyls feed their babies?'

Max didn't – none of his books at home had ever said anything about it. 'No. How?'

'They chew the food up and then spit it into the baby's mouth.'

'Yuck!' Max pulled a face. 'That's gross!'

Reg squawked and snapped his beak again.

Fern's eyes sparkled wickedly. 'I think your baby's waiting to be fed!'

'Oh, no! No way!' said Max, shaking his head vigorously.

'Yummy fish, Max.' Fern held up the plate to him teasingly. 'Come on, feed your little baby!'

But no matter how cute Reg was, Max wasn't about to chew up a piece of raw fish and spit it into his mouth! He frowned. He couldn't leave the pterodactyl hungry.

I know! he thought.

He mashed the fish up with his thumb then held it in his fingers and swooped it down towards the little pterodactyl, like a

mother bird with food in her beak.

'Open wide!' he cried.

The baby gave a delighted 'Caaaaark!' and opened his beak so wide Max could see all the way down his throat. Max popped the food in and then whisked his hand out of the way before the beak shut. He didn't want his fingers to be part of the pterodactyl's lunch!

It took quite a while to feed Reg *and* eat his own lunch, but at last Max finished and helped Fern clear up. Adam still wasn't back.

'What do you think we should do now?' asked Max.

'Maybe we could make a start on training Reg?' suggested Fern.

Max nodded. 'Good idea.'

They went outside. 'So, how are we going to do it?' Max said.

'I've been thinking, why don't we go somewhere away from the house and try throwing him into the air?' said Fern. 'Once he's high up he might remember what to do.'

Max wasn't totally convinced but he couldn't think of a better plan. He lifted Reg on to his shoulder. Then they ran down the path, past the ponds and swamps, and the paddocks and barns that made up the sanctuary, until they found a quiet spot by the hay barn.

'OK, here you go, Reg,' said Max. He took the pterodactyl off his shoulder and flung him into the air.

Reg gave a startled squawk. He fell like a stone for a few seconds, then he flapped his wings frantically and managed to land back on Max's shoulder.

Max tried again, throwing him even higher. Reg flapped his wings harder but still circled round and came back.

'He just doesn't want to leave you, does he?' said Fern.

Max shook his head.

'No luck?' a voice called from the path. It

was Adam, riding on Trixie's back. Trixie was a large brown and green einiosaurus with four sturdy legs and a long tail. She looked a lot like a triceratops but her central horn curved down instead of up. Seeing Max, she bellowed in delight. She stopped beside him and pushed him gently with her horn in greeting.

'Hey, Trixie,' Max said, hugging her. 'I've missed you!' He scratched the dinosaur's head and she snorted and gave a happy sigh.

'So, how's it going with Reg?' asked Adam.

'Not great,' admitted Fern. 'He flies a little way up, but he keeps coming back to Max. Perhaps Max needs to learn to fly!'

Adam's eyes gleamed. 'Hmm, now maybe I could invent something . . .'

'No, Dad!' said Fern hastily.

'There must be *something* else we can do,' said Max, wracking his brains. 'If only we could get him higher still.'

'Wait a minute!' Fern stared at Trixie,

her eyes brightening. 'I've just thought of something. Have you finished with Trixie for the afternoon, Dad?'

'Yes,' said Adam, wrinkling his brow.

'Can we borrow her?' asked Fern.

'Borrow her?' said Adam. 'Whatever for?'

'We could take Reg for a ride, out on to the open plains,' said Fern. 'If we canter, the wind might remind Reg of flying and encourage him to take off into the skies from Trixie's back.'

Adam looked doubtful. 'Well, I suppose it's worth a try, although I'm not sure that's going to be your answer.'

'It *might* work,' said Max, who was longing to have a ride on Trixie again.

Fern grinned and took Trixie's reins from her dad. 'What are we waiting for? Let's go!'

Pterodactyl in Peril!

Trixie knelt down and Fern mounted. Max climbed up behind her with Reg still clinging to his shoulder. Fern picked up the reins, gave Trixie a quick nudge with her heels, and they went lumbering out of the sanctuary. Reg squawked in surprise.

'See you later, Dad,' Fern shouted.

'Be careful,' Adam called back.

'We will!' Max and Fern headed out across the bumpy ground of the plains. Fern nudged Trixie into a trot. Soon they were bouncing along, trying not to slip off the einiosaurus's

broad back. Reg opened his wings halfway, struggling to balance. He screeched excitedly and jiggled from one foot to the other. But the faster the einiosaurus thundered across the plains, the tighter the pterodactyl clung to Max.

'He's not flying off yet!' gasped Max. 'And his talons are sharp!'

'Faster, Trixie!' Fern cried, gently coaxing the einiosaurus into a gallop. 'Go on, Reg, fly!'

But it didn't make any difference.

Finally, exhausted, Trixie slowed down and stopped in the shade of a pine tree at the base of the smoking volcano. Max was very glad. His shoulder was sore with the weight of Reg – and from his sharp talons!

Max and Fern jumped down from Trixie's back. Max moved Reg across to his other shoulder.

'Well, that didn't work,' said Fern, disappointed. 'What do we do *now*?'

Max looked round for ideas. There wasn't anything nearby apart from the tree arching over them . . .

The tree! Of course!

'I know!' he exclaimed. 'How about I climb the tree with Reg?'

'Um . . . why?' Fern looked puzzled.

'I'll show you!' said Max.

Excitedly, Max started to climb the tree with Reg still on his shoulder. There were plenty of low branches at the bottom that he could use for hand and footholds.

As Max pulled himself up, Reg flapped his wings. 'It's all right,' Max soothed. He grinned to himself. He never thought he'd be climbing a tree with a pterodactyl on his shoulder!

'Be careful, Max!' Fern called from below. 'You're getting quite high.'

'I have to!' he called back. 'The higher the better!'

Near to the top, Max edged on to a sturdy branch. He wiggled into a safe position with his legs on either side of the branch and his back leaning against the rough, solid trunk. Then he carefully lifted Reg off his shoulder.

Reg seemed to know what Max planned to do. He flapped frantically and tried to climb back up Max's arm.

'Oh no you don't!' said Max. 'Go on, you can fly from this tree. You can do it!' He tried to throw Reg into the air.

But the pterodactyl clung on even more tightly with its claws and screeched in Max's ear.

'Go on!' Max cried.

'It's very sweet that he likes you so much!' said Fern from down below.

'Sweet?' Max shouted back. 'It's not

sweet. He's *got* to fly!'

He placed Reg gently on to one of the
branches and began to climb back down.

'What are you doing?' Fern called.

'Seeing what happens if I leave him alone
up there,' said Max.

Max reached the ground quickly and looked up. Reg stared down at him unhappily. Max flapped his arms up and down.

Fern creased up laughing as Reg put his head on one side and gave a puzzled squawk.

'It's not funny!' Max cried.

'Oh, it is!' said Fern. She flapped her own arms to imitate him.

A grin caught at Max's mouth. He picked up a pine cone and threw it lightly at Fern. She squealed and threw one back. Reg watched them from above, his eyes wide. 'Caaarrrrrk!' he said.

'So, what now?' said Fern after a while. 'We can't just leave him up there and he doesn't look like he's about to fly away.'

They stared at the baby pterodactyl. Max

felt completely stumped.

Suddenly he spotted something flying towards the tree. He screwed up his eyes against the bright light of the sun. What was it? As the creature got closer, Max saw that it was a large winged dinosaur – a pterosaur of some sort – with a red and yellow head, a vicious-looking beak and huge wings. Its body was as long as a double-decker bus.

'It's enormous!' cried Fern, as the predator glided towards them. Its wings looked at least

twelve metres long. It screamed savagely and they saw the sharp teeth lining its beak.

'It's a quetzalcoatlus!' gasped Max.

'A quetza-what?' said Fern.

'A quetzalcoatlus,' said Max. 'Try saying it bit by bit: quet . . . zal . . . co . . . at . . . lus. It's a meat-eating pterosaur!'

'Oh no!' said Fern, standing stock-still, terrified, as the gigantic creature swooped towards them.

Max felt an icy jolt run through him as he realized the predator's vicious black eyes were fixed on Reg.

The creature swooped hungrily at the tree.

'Quick, Reg. Fly!' Fern shrieked.

It was as if everything was happening in slow motion . . . the pterosaur dived for the baby pterodactyl, who sat marooned on the branch.

'We've got to do something, Max,' wailed Fern.

Max raced to the bottom of the tree. In seconds, he was climbing up and up, one branch after the other.

'I didn't mean that!' gasped Fern. 'Come

down! You'll get eaten!'

But Max couldn't stand by and watch the pterosaur grab Reg. 'Reg! Come here!' he called.

It was too late. Just as Max reached the branch below the one where Reg was perched, the quetzalcoatlus grabbed the baby pterodactyl in its sharp talons.

Max's heart somersaulted. 'No!' he yelled. He jumped and grabbed on to Reg's tail. The huge pterosaur flapped away from the tree, taking Reg – and Max – with it.

'Max!' screamed Fern, as Max and Reg swung wildly from the quetzalcoatlus's giant claws!

Up, up and Away!

Max felt the wind whistling past his face. He yelled. His weight was dragging the pterosaur down – they were going to hit the ground hard, and Reg would get hurt.

Reg was screeching in terror. Max swung his body up and grabbed one of the giant pterosaur's bony legs so he wasn't pulling on Reg's tail any more.

'It's all right. It's going to be OK,' he gasped to the frightened baby.

'Max! Let go!' yelled Fern from beneath him.

'I can't. I'm not leaving Reg!' Max shouted. His muscles hurt but he hung on tightly.

'You have to!'

'No. It'll come back down to the ground soon.' *I hope,* he added in his head.

But the pterosaur began to flap its massive

wings in earnest and started to fly higher.

Max's arms felt like they were going to come off! *What am I going to do?* he thought as he saw the blue sky above him.

Suddenly, something hit the pterosaur's belly, just above Max's head.

Max twisted round and saw that Fern had mounted Trixie and was chasing after him. She had an armful of big fir cones and was urging Trixie into a lumbering gallop.

'Faster, Trixie . . . faster,' she called. 'It's all right, Max! I'm coming after you!'

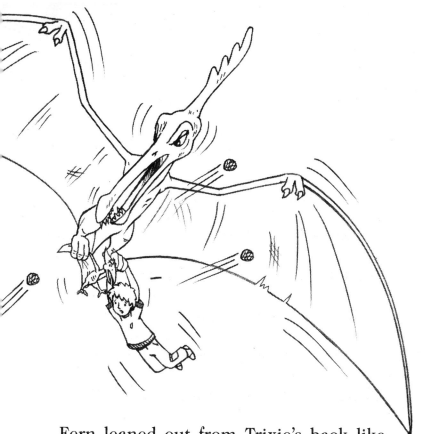

Fern leaned out from Trixie's back like a rodeo-rider and, taking aim, she threw another fir cone as hard as she could at the pterosaur.

PING! The fir cone hit the flying dinosaur's neck and bounced off. The pterosaur gave an angry shriek and swung its head down, glaring at Fern. She took no notice. She just threw another fir cone.

The giant bird swooped lower. 'Caaaark!' it screeched furiously as a fir cone found a soft bit of underbelly. Fern was a great shot!

Suddenly, the pterosaur seemed to decide it had had enough of the painful missiles and the extra weight. It opened its talons and let

Max and Reg go.

Max shouted as he felt himself fall. His heart was in his mouth. Down and down he went until . . . thump! He landed in the middle of a leafy bush. Branches scratched at his face and arms, but at least he was safe. He struggled to sit up as Fern cantered over on Trixie.

'Are you all right?' she exclaimed.

'I'm fine, but where's Reg?'

Fern looked very relieved to see Max

safely back on the ground. 'There he is. Look!' She pointed upwards. 'He seems to have remembered how to fly!'

When the big pterosaur had dropped Reg, he hadn't fallen to the ground. Instead, Reg had flapped his wings and now he was flying in a circle above them. He was calling

anxiously, his eyes searching round. As he saw Max scramble out of the bush he gave a delighted screech and swooped down to land on his shoulder.

'Oh, Reg! You're safe!' said Max.

'Caaark!' said the pterodactyl, nibbling his ear in a friendly way.

'And we know he can fly properly now,' said Fern. 'Go on, Reg. Fly away.'

But the pterodactyl just settled more firmly on Max's shoulder. Max stroked him, feeling grateful that he and Reg were both in one piece.

'What are we going to do with him?' sighed Fern. 'We have to find a way of making him fly back to his flock.'

Max frowned. Fern was right. It was the only way Reg would be able to live safely and happily.

'We'll think of something,' Max said,

hoping he was right.

'I suppose we'd better go back and tell Dad that our idea didn't work,' Fern said. She and Max climbed back on Trixie and set off for home.

As they rode into the sanctuary, they saw Adam working on the windmill. He had taken it apart and now all the pieces lay scattered around him on the ground.

'Hi, Dad!' Fern called.

Adam looked up. 'Oh, hi, you two! No success then?' he said, nodding at Reg.

'Er, no,' said Fern, shooting Max a look. 'Not really. We did get him to fly a bit but we couldn't make him fly away.'

'I thought you might find that,' Adam said. 'Now, about this windmill. Do you think it could be the way I tied the sails on?' He pointed at a bolt on the ground. 'Perhaps they were just too tight?'

'I doubt it would be that,' said Max,

jumping down from Trixie. 'Do you want us to help you put the windmill back together?'

'Good idea.' As Adam hammered in the pole again and attached the wheel, Max and Fern hung up the pieces of sack cloth. There was a light breeze in the air. When it was all done, they stood back hopefully. Would the sails turn? But still nothing.

'Perhaps we could try moving it to a different position?' said Max.

'I've tried that once already and it didn't

make any difference,' Adam said gloomily. The frustration was clearly getting the better of him. 'Oh, I give up! I think we'd better call it a day. It's starting to get dark anyway.'

It was true. As Max looked around him, he realized that night was starting to set in.

'Why don't you go and get Reg settled into an enclosure,' said Adam. 'Then come in and get some supper. A good night's sleep might help us think better tomorrow.'

Max was excited. It would be the first

time he'd ever actually stayed the night in Dinosaur Land! He thought for a moment that his mum and dad might get worried, but then he remembered that no time passed in his world while he was away.

Max and Fern took Reg to one of the barns. The pterodactyl didn't want to leave Max's side at first, but finally he settled down in some hay. He gave a tired 'caaaark!' and then tucked his head under one leathery wing and went to sleep.

After supper, Max, Fern and Adam got ready to go to sleep too. There were basic wooden beds piled high with blankets and furs to keep warm.

Adam blew out the candles that were lighting the stone house.

Max lay there in the dark. His first sleepover in Dinosaur Land should have been really exciting, but he couldn't *properly* enjoy it because he was worrying so much about Reg. What were they going to do with him? Thoughts spun around Max's head until finally his eyes drifted shut . . .

Problems Solved!

When Max woke the next morning, it was just starting to get light. He couldn't think where he was for a moment. But then he saw Fern's tousled curly hair and heard Adam's loud snores and he remembered. He was in Dinosaur Land, of course! He lay quite still, thinking again about Reg and his flock . . .

His flock! Max sat bolt upright in bed. Maybe that was it. He remembered that Jenny the farm park owner had said that the owl chick she had fostered with a hen hadn't flown properly until it saw the other owls flying around. Maybe if Reg saw his flock again he'd start acting like them and fly off?

'Fern! Fern!' Max rocked his sleeping friend's shoulder. 'I've had an idea! About Reg!'

'What is it?' Adam sat up on the other

side of the room and stretched his arms out.

Quickly, Max explained the theory about the owl chick.

'Hmm, it's certainly an idea,' said Adam thoughtfully. 'The pterodactyls will still be fairly close by – they stay by a lake and then fly on in a few weeks.'

'So can we try, Dad?' asked Fern.

'Definitely,' Adam nodded. 'I'll try anything to help a dinosaur.'

The three of them dressed quickly and

went outside. In no time at all they had Trixie ready and were heading out of the sanctuary into the early morning sun. Reg was balanced carefully on Max's shoulder. Max breathed in deep lungfuls of the clear air. Was this going to work?

They rode across the plains to the lake. As they got near, they heard the faint sound of cawing and saw some black specks in the sky. The noise gradually got louder and louder until the specks took the shape

of pterodactyls. They were flying off the ground, circling in the sky and swooping down to the water to catch fish.

'Caaaarkk . . . caaaarkk . . . caaarkkkk . . .' Max felt Reg bob up and down in excitement as he saw his flock.

Adam pulled Trixie to a sharp halt.

Reg squawked loudly and flapped his wings. The pterodactyls overhead were making a deafening noise now. Reg jumped up slightly into the air, then landed back down on Max's shoulders. He stretched his wings out again. Then he nuzzled Max's cheek with his beak and looked upwards at the dinosaurs in the sky. It was as if he was asking Max to fly too.

'I can't come with you, Reg,' Max said softly.

Reg pulled at Max's hair impatiently.

'No, you have to go on your own,' Max said, feeling a little lump in his throat. He stroked Reg. 'Please go. You'll be happier with your flock. I can't stay here forever.'

For a brief moment, pterodactyl and boy looked at each other and then, with a giant flap of his wings, Reg flew up into the sky.

Max swallowed as he watched him go. His eyes followed Reg as he flew around with the flock, but soon he had lost sight of him.

'He's gone,' said Max. He felt happy but

sad at the same time.

Adam turned and squeezed his shoulder. 'He's back where he belongs and it's all thanks to you, Max.'

Fern smiled. 'Look, there he is!' She pointed at a small pterodactyl shooting down from the sky into the water before flying up again with a silver fish in its beak.

'Bye, Reg!' Max called.

As he watched the pterodactyl fly away to join the others, something dawned on him.

'Look at his wings, Adam!'

'What about them?' asked Adam, squinting into the sky.

'Don't you see?' said Max excitedly. 'They're not flat to the wind. They're at an angle. Maybe if we put the windmill sails at an angle it might work – they might start moving.'

Adam stared at him. 'You know, I think you could be right!' he said. 'This could be it! This might just do the trick!'

They couldn't wait to get to the sanctuary to see if that was the solution to the windmill problem. Trixie cantered all the way, her passengers swaying from side to side with each lumbering stride.

As soon as they arrived, they all jumped off. Adam adjusted the sails on the windmill so that they were at an angle and then he stood back.

Max held his breath as the wind blew and then . . . slowly, ever so slowly, the sails started to move. He couldn't believe his eyes as the wind picked up and the sails started spinning, faster and faster.

'It's working!' Fern cried. 'Oh, Max, you did it!'

Adam enveloped Max and Fern in a big bear hug. 'This is brilliant! Now we'll have water whenever we, or the dinosaurs, need it!'

'I'm really glad it's working,' said Max. He watched the sails going round and thought

about Reg swooping through the sky. Both

problems had been solved! Relief rushed

through him . . . and just in time too! At that

moment, there was a loud humming sound

and his pocket began to feel very hot.

'The fossil!' he cried out. 'I think I'm going home!'

'Bye, Max!' cried Fern. 'I hope you come back soon!'

'Me too!' said Max. 'Bye!'

A wave of colours surrounded him and he tumbled away . . .

When Max came back down to land, he rubbed his eyes. The vast plains of Dinosaur

Land had been replaced with the small fields of Meadow Farm Park.

Max saw the henhouse and pond. No time had passed in his own world. The mother hen was still frantically clucking and flapping her wings as the baby duckling paddled round in the water. She thought the duckling was about to drown! Max knew he couldn't explain to the hen that the duckling would be all right and he hated seeing her so upset. He ran over and reached out his hand.

The duckling swam into it. Max placed the tiny creature back with the hen on dry land. She held up her wings and it ran to nestle under them, peeping out at Max.

Max grinned. 'I think you'd better keep your swimming trips for when your new

mum isn't around,' he told the duckling.

'What's going on here?'

Max turned to see his mum and Jenny. He explained what had happened with the duckling.

'The poor hen must have been very upset,' said his mum.

'Thanks for helping out, Max,' said Jenny.

Max's mum ruffled his hair. 'You love helping animals, don't you, Max?'

Max nodded. *And dinosaurs too,* he

added in his head. He thought about Reg
flying happily with his flock in Dinosaur
Land. Perhaps he'd see him again one day.
And he couldn't wait to go back and see Fern
and Adam too. Curling his fingers around
the fossil in his pocket, Max smiled.